ALL THE LAVISH IN COMMON

Also by Allan Peterson—

Anonymous Or

CHAPBOOKS
Any Given Moment
Speechless
Small Charities
Stars on a Wire

ALL THE LAVISH IN COMMON

Allan Peterson

University of Massachusetts Press   *Amherst and Boston*

Copyright 2006 by
University of Massachusetts Press
All rights reserved
Printed in the
United States of America

LC 2005036571
ISBN 1-55849-526-6

Designed by Sally Nichols
Set in Monotype Bell
Printed and bound by
Thomson-Shore, Inc.

Library of Congress Cataloging-in-Publication Data

Peterson, Allan.
  All the lavish in common : poems / Allan Peterson.
    p. cm.
  "Winner of the 2005 Juniper Prize for Poetry."
  ISBN 1-55849-526-6 (pbk. : alk. paper)
  I. Title.
  PS3566.E7647A45 2006
  811'.6—dc22

                                        2005036571

British Library Cataloguing in Publication data are available.

MORE IS MORE

ACKNOWLEDGMENTS

Grateful acknowledgment is made to the following journals
in which these poems first appeared:

"How Folklore Starts," *Agni*

"Bone Structure," *Arts & Letters*

"As Far As," *Big City Lit*

"Wind Chill," *Brown Box*

"Sad Facts," *Eclipse*

"How Far Behind We Are," "I'll Take It from Here," *EDGZ*

"Critical Mass," *Epoch*

"Spontaneous Combustion," "Bunji," *Georgetown Review*

"Holding Your Horses," "The Need to Explain," "Virtues," *Green Mountains Review*

"One Day in Texas History," *Gulf Coast*

"Going Gooseflesh," *Gulf Stream Magazine*

"Reluctant," *Into the Teeth of the Wind*

"June in the Inner Ear," *Literal Latté*

"Before the Afterlife," *No Exit*

"Living in Minutes," *Pleiades*

"Cosmology," "Heroic Proportions," "Swallowtails," "Back to Us Last Night," "Under Oath," *The Adirondack Review*

"I Swear," *The Chattahoochee Review*

"Taking My Time," *The Comstock Review*

"The Surface of Europa," *The Farmer's Market*

"What Belongs," *The Lullwater Review*

"Where Should I Begin," "Private Lives,"* "An Anecdote," *The Montserrat Review*

"Taking for Instance," *The Sonora Review*

"Solemn Examples," *The Southern Anthology 1995*

"What Refill Means," *The Southern Anthology 1996*

"Breathing without Exhales," *Water-Stone*

* Nominated for Pushcart Prize

CONTENTS

ALL THE LAVISH IN COMMON

WHERE SHOULD I BEGIN

I am statistical and not
as they used to say about Amelia
a long drink of water
In the history of large behaviors I am not mentioned
In the small I am equally left out
On the last train to maximize disorder
my car sits on a siding my bags go on without me
labeled density and pressure
It's nothing personal I am not diminished
It cannot be worse than this neutral
the point beyond which disarrangement cannot go
I cannot begin to tell you
how this morning touching the oak
cracked in half by the hurricane that did not even hit here
directly but flattened Mississippi
I found it soft I made it waver with a touch
Years of fungus beetles and woodpeckers
had turned it to sponge
So I grew it back in my mind like one of the pleasures
of early schoolhood
getting the AV boys to run the films backward in Hygiene
or Sociology and the water disappeared
the children at school backed once more into their houses
and were wrapped again in their bedcovers
Bedouins returned to their tents
to refill their glasses with tea from their own mouths
And it was not true that I cannot begin to tell you
I can I cannot finish I mean

PRIVATE LIVES

How orb-weavers patch up the air in places
like fibrinogen, or live in the fence lock.
How the broom holds lizards.
How if you stand back you will miss them
afflicted by sunset,
the digger bees mining the yard,
birds too fast to have shadows,
the life that lives in the wren whistle.
You will see moth-clouds
that are moving breaths
and perhaps something like the star
that fell on Alabama
through the roof of Mrs. E. Hulitt Hodges
and hit her radio, then her.
No, you must be close for the real story.
I remember being made
to stand in the corner for punishment
because it would be dull and empty
and I would be sorry.
But instead it was a museum of small wonders,
a place of three walls
with a weather my breath influenced,
an archaeology of layers, of painted molding,
a meadow as we called them then
of repeatable pale roses,
an eight-eyed spider in a tear of wallpaper
turning my corner.
The texture. The soft echo if I talked,
if I said I am not bad if this is the world.

BLACKOUT WITH HERBS

Light behind clouds is like corn starch
that thickens gravy.
The effect is so delicious we forget the calendar
also needs extra days like a pinch of cilantro,
how often someone is explaining how unlikely it was
so many things could have gone wrong at the same time.
Did and do with some regularity,
as when the West Coast went dark like a sauce
at Aroma of Mandarin when a bird in the rafters
spooked by watchmen startled a squirrel
that turned in a space too tight between power lines
and California looked like a fast blanket
pulled across the hills.

It is good to review how likely the impossible is
those things even beyond consideration, impregnation
of the earth by meteors, whereby metals rooted and grew
to be harvested like basil and oregano,
or were thought of as viscous rivers to be traced
and forded underground like the Rio Plata.
I have not had a dream of flying in two years,
not since I sailed from the walls of Siena
after *lasagna al forno e un mezzo litro di vino da tavola*
and visited the fields of Chianti and back
to see the old souls again in the cathedral where upstairs
in the treasury the impossibly lonesome bones
are arranged like salads.

THE SURFACE OF EUROPA

I call your attention to the surface of Europa
and my dimpled heels
a connection plain as the fact of an overcoat thrown
over heaven and we see the moth holes
but draw the conclusion while our cage is dark
we should stop singing
and sit quietly despite the outside rage of objects
and the fact the intuitive
still has primacy over the technical

While my head rests on my arm I can think
I am a bird with prismatic bones
I do not need space ships to study this connection
A vacuum is just an idea
in which I can still breathe normally
With the light behind me
I write in the shadow of my hand don't see
what I am saying I think by feel
I feel by think I float down supported by the rarest
of atmospheres—no atmosphere
I grow from a glob to an oval in my O's
like an egg pressured by oviduct
diagrams orbits
foot-dragging bubbles in the wing of a dragonfly

ELEMENTARITY

In the almost unkeepable archives of recall
I think it was Robert Billingsly
who after learning of the muon and meson
discovered the hardon
as both easily detectable and basic and years later
following his bubbles
through a school of silversides off Santa Barbara
large as a car lot
watched how they formed around him a thinking rose
So he added the singular
hard factors of astonishment to his basic elements
and began to imagine
how combinations of these particles might create a world
where venality was not recompensed
deep pleasure was constant and not disgraceful
the ephemeral was eternally resident
though seen glimpsingly and sympathy became common
as silver fish forming an aster
suggesting the appearance of a single mind
So when the car in Clearwater
was pulled over because it appeared to the officer
an iguana was driving
both hands on the wheel though his owner as a prank
had merely slouched down
he thought it was just another extensive etcetera
the charges of which are neutral though nonetheless electric

FROM THE HEART

To say it right you would have to gather the printers of Meriden
Connecticut and of Basel
paper makers from Twin Rocker ink grinders cuttlefish and soy
metalflake lapis suspended in oil
typecutters calligraphers applicators rubricators floralized reps
from tattoo parlors who are talking pictures
You would use only small letters since you mean soft and intimate
use plain water but natural not tap
that with spat and barnacles nauplia zoea zooplankters hydroids
more varied than intruding vessels from science fiction
a phrase like pigmy mammoths
two ospreys whose doubles float below them for miles
pidgins dialects jargons creoles
rebus acrostic and seven down the nine letter word for outnumber
Nothing is simple but what we choose to ignore
like the ciliated tufts in the oviducts of a mouse waving like grass
seasonal variations in salinity
If nature is all we have the god-noun that encompasses everything
and I am of it since it cannot be otherwise
then everything I imagine is and all scrutinized day night or afternoon
on the knobby couch and bumper flash
from Nancy's classic Thunderbird This is the message:
Of love letters in English there are 26 and feelings outnumber flies

SWALLOWTAILS

The Emperor thought of his heart as a water wheel
flooding the rice fields of all creation
and bloodied the water for a better harvest.
His warriors hoped for a life with wings.
His swallowtails wrote him the same lines
—the secret of life is a resurrected worm—
He told them eventually time would run backwards
in their hands, now empty where a crossbow went.

A theory works if it answers the exceptions.
The writing in the air of swallowtails,
from here to where the time changes at Mexico Beach,
is like writing all the armies of the afterlife
waiting underground in China.

We are attuned to shadows. They strafe the shore.
An osprey spins above the trees.
But when a large one stops suddenly above the house,
all the laws have been broken.
A theory that a moment is a warehouse where armies are stacked
to the ceiling, then one falls, is the last exception.
The osprey's underside is streaked like a zebra swallowtail.
It misses the fish that dove out of the reach of shadows
as the lovers jumped into theirs from the Bay Bridge in Fort Walton.
If any should meet hovering over a milkweed or reflection,
they might say didn't I know you in another life,
the kind of thing said often in Fort Walton or the Orient
and didn't plum blossoms freeze in the Emperor's courtyard.

TRANSFUSION

I have written it five times or more, each uneasy.
Drafts, as if wind blew uncomfortably through and the loose door chattered,
the toilet spoke with its moan voice, the deep pipes shuddering.
After a long wait trying to remember his name,
I touched the phone book and it came without opening.
I felt a chill.
Then I wondered the whereabouts of the South Star
since a North existed and touched the Ephemeris. Nothing. No one had.
Another symmetry misspoke.
And for the second time Terry's own blood left the table,
swirled through the room and tubing before return.
Imagine its migration in a single room,
petrels in the blood from far away as South America.
After the machinery it came back.
You could hear it like the whump of wind refilling sails to the shapes of colters
on the way to the self-centered idea of the New World,
well, new to some Spanish.
But it was the same world, now in miniature, the masts relaxed
in their neck rings, then teased up on ropes like a path to the Western Ocean
which was the Eastern Ocean
through a miracle of circuitry and cruelties.
In the last draft the patient became an explorer through his blood
which traveled in pinwheels though he stayed put, whirlpools,
all aspects of weather on a sphere which revels but does not survive,
and the story almost unrecognized from where it started.

TODAY THE SWALLOWS

Today the swallows wrote Shakespeare in the air.
           I saw sonnet after sonnet, swooping exhunts, pulled curtains.
Last night a tanager sat learning its wings in my hand.
        It took minutes. Next I was waking
to bells light as feathers.
          So this poem will be a relic layered with sorrow like its kind,
hand over hand, sedimentary accrual the top of which is compromise
with the happy ending, the ceiling, the roof with its wings on downstroke,
the home symbolically leaving,
          so abandonment is an everyday fact encompassing how long
it took to live after it, by which time most have achieved obscurity,
the distance from the sun to its flower, my head whose sutures
are arranged like a comic dawn.

At once the trees were beaded with leaf buds,
          April unbuttoning May.
In no time the empty yard was full, covered over,
          the expanse become a tunnel, plywood turning
framing into walls.
In no time we are convinced we have memories,
          that somewhere the brain records everything,
that timeless often drags on, reasons traced to trees and savannas,
caves and ice-blocks.
          At the same time we think ourselves unique, heirs to almost nothing
but blue eyes and hair, dim skin
on which we have pinpricked symbols as reasons, reminders,
          like seeing sky twice, one birdless and empty,
one almost metrically alive.

VISCOSITY

You remember poets those that write tangibly
about the intangibles
the way confident water softens red beans overnight
just by conviction,
onions whose pale dresses keep slipping off
despite their shy vegetability,
that provide a planetarium inside a planetarium
where their science sees what's missing
—dark matter—and compares it to a backyard pond
with black mollies so we'll understand;
who were some of the first to notice the sketch
more satisfying than the finished
painting, that dreams induce lightning and the like,
that pages despite desperate messages
turned yellow on the shelves, whether handled or ignored.

Yes to eons, out of print illustrations, yes to the innocent
ginkoes, the confiscated shadows
whereby even in December it is summer by the lamps
and we linger there,
the dust like diatoms in the salty ocean falling slowly,
hanging suspended, laden though they are,
a choir convincing a forest of hands in the molecules
to lift them.
When I first saw Frances in the printmaking studio
at Southern Illinois,
the light shafts began to solidify, the tray of nitric tightened
to its bubbles, the room thickened
and stayed with me.
Now after forty years nothing aromatic has reached the ceiling,
nothing then falling reached the floor.
It is the kind of thing like mind and resemblance you'd say
are merely opinions,
but it's still three in the afternoon and she's still turning
younger toward the door.

HOW FAR BEHIND WE ARE

Not just the downbeat and retrieval of the heart,
this developed much earlier and involved the octopus
smart as a dog, Spaniel smart as a pig,
horse smart as a … well now you've got me,
maybe the Music Volute printing symphonies outright on its shell.

Stories began to involve someone being two places at once,
having conversations with a broom,
someone showing a gold thigh at Biblos and Tyre
in a single afternoon.

No one ever considered things to be that widespread.
Even arithmologists who value counting, underestimated straw.

Ordinarily the occipital decides, when sunlight makes a face on water
and the wind draws in a beard and wild hair,
or you sit in a dark room and stars assemble their oncoming Pontiacs.

We are hungered by images.
We feed mutually after we make them.
We can comb out the face with our thoughts,
make out maps to a treasure on the wings of a Checkerspot.
We gather the animals dressed in flowers and music,
we open their throats since they do not pretend higher purpose.

This is how far behind we are. Our mysteries. Our little ignorance.
Rituals made of nothing but surprise,
as when gardenias burn in one's presence just by touch.

TRIAL

Nothing more poignant than a being trying
to understand itself,
than a being helping another with no understanding
other than need, nothing more
than a being knowing something, caring for something
incapable of care,
than one caring for knowing so that care might be
available when needed,
when need is not wonder but a being itself.

Our myths were Indians though this was not India.
We ruined them obsessively.
Now farms. We crush the small ones and poison
the larger, all wistlessly.
In the jurisdiction of humiliation we are peerless.
Magniloquent. Eating our own.
In dislike and loathing are no honeymoons.
A man covered in bird feathers, a field feathered with corn.
Each could overcome us
and so defeat endless successions of threats,
endemic to out of date worlds.

The arid climate of exclusion rots leather armor.
Shock strikes quietly.
Aiders and abettors are conspicuously forgiven.
The rooftop would be opened like tent flaps,
legends rewritten in the fields.
Black water would argue against us.
Enter the alkaloids.
Enter water and electrolytes. Too much and too little.
Causality going one way, morality the other,
hiding their eyes.

AMPLE EVIDENCE

An unlikely man in a black dress insisted
the summoned bodies would appear in Paradise
leaving their bones behind
for which there was ample evidence
But that meant the thus-blessed were destined
to be helpless jellies before the Throne
unacceptable except to the truly forlorn past participle
of the verb *to lose*
an obeisance undignified for a people that made time
a common province of machines and music
a handiwork impossible for the contents of a gourd

Take a likely someone in his off-hours
that might travel from the Newark Clock Shop to the Apollo
just to hear heavenly voices storing daylight and grandeur
sing his bones alive
Something accomplished elaborately is devotion
like the few dozen hours it takes to make a watch
whose wheels are engraved with flourishes
or the years the four live harmonizers
The Spiders who recorded for Atlantic back in the 50's
stood together pointing upward shoveling spinning in unison
as if the music could be wound up be sewn to the living air
to make it last and whose audiences chimed like clockwork

LANDMARKS

None at sea. In each moment a thousand crowns,
and miters, and ocean in consternation
in a movie of mountain building, the earth speeded up,
a stirring from underneath of cullet
as if the wind was inward and the sense was symptom.
This is the instant before death, eyes brimming,
when everything flashes before you
as it's flashing now, taking a lifetime to use up
the expanded moments, the fractal panorama,
the dilemma of together and aloof.
Her grandfather announced he was preparing,
putting his letters in order when he turned too late
at the mailbox as the handbrake failed.
The car rolled forward with predictable results.
His wife's cries flattened the foothills to dead calm.

Sometimes the ocean is roiling men,
silver in breastplates and greaves, shingles for the shins,
horizon to horizon, lost relatives among them.
They are learning, but too late.
Duration is like blood to time, the river in which it swims.
But that is not what the sea believes. It answers one hard,
endless and blameless.
But since it lost the nine sailors of the *Cindy Brent*,
no one believes the story of misplacing its islands,
losing its way like the rest of us.

AN ANECDOTE

sounds like a cure for something
but is a little revelation
like mute one morning after the stroke he woke up
to see all the children
flown in with nieces nephews interchangeable husbands
and uttered his first words
O my goodness
suddenly knowing it was downhill from there.
When I went out the back door
of the last room at Lake Quinault into the hillside forest
of salal and discovery
and found signs and markers identifying trees
and native vegetation
it was like a family gathering. There was a danger
of losing everything.
I should have taken Raymond Bluefield a local to tell me
the names and how Miriam
his daughter was spoken to by spiders how the elk appeared
as his father to say he was leaving
for good for the Olympic forest how in his double-ender
now he feels like Mary of the Moon
and I might say stop. Pay no attention to the rest.
Sometimes Blue Jays will scold us
to the whole outdoors though we are only refilling the feeder.
The real details are the unexpected
taking on new life. None of us can tell when children gather
or leave or where or what we may do
with our intentions our useless medicine at the last minute.

BONE STRUCTURE

Lint is the end of things, and bones, algae and refusal
to accept new evidence of the last world or the next.
      Fish bones, a puzzle of shatters like broken glass,
a clock impossible to wind or rebuild without parts left over,
mirror images of *no* and *on*, a spine cascading like a flight of stairs.
      Every bone with its dark-finned shark process swimming
relentlessly through daylight.

Now the Willet with the limp is back
after escaping the Sharp-shinned. Now there are pen lines for veins
and unequal footprints, water copying their eyes.
      Now the landscape is long breaths and nine muscles
enter quietly the thumb, the lace of the chain link
beautifies the lawn.
      Now the dancer who was a jeweler by day
and the gemstone that was a dancer by night, are waiting
for coils to vermillionize the stove.
Who will speak first of the fall of '85. How many objects
remind them of time lost to each other, limbs lost, letters.
A with its legs widespread, *F* with its ligatures

      And the falls since, each recollection paying for shadows
on the white page, cream page, bone between,
white only by comparison and favoring one leg,
      shifting weight, uneasy in dead silence.
Behind them the Coldspot was dropping its ice cubes
      like femurs and phalanges out of danger
behind the sturdy and insulated door.

TRESPASS

The recent was so enough, I quit.
What more was there, anyway.
As it is in Arkansas, so it is in English,
but the outcomes are more complicated.
The arc of minutes in the sky over Hot Springs
left plenty. So much, I decided, was self-evident.
For instance, one lung is smaller than the other.
The reason is the heart
which is not quite middle, but the left.
The same side on which I hear superior.

In reading *The Illustrated Wasps of Ireland,*
I heard our shared wrens so loud I sat
bolt upright into the loads of listening.
Which is more pathetic, those winged children,
innocent infants of the times, or horoscopes,
whose front pages equal the news of Zambia
or Bonn.

Dragging out the photographs of Mao
swimming the Yangtze,
he has been there so long without moving
he must be puckered beyond belief.
So answer the telescope, ring up the distant
and disharmonious families. You see our problem.
There are so many of us now, and we are lying.

VIRTUES

Because William Tell was just a remake of Abraham and Isaac
and both lucked out out of arrogance and obedience
because all flowers are black at night and the object-lesson sons
who were only ideas about whose is whose and how much one is
willing to lose for the sake of sheer instruction Do as I say or else
Like they liked to repeat in art school about a given composition
how the eye is *led* like a puppy from the cup to the window
to the painter with the rolled newspaper
Out the window we think there is a globe tugged on by a moon
but the lake does not move under it It is still there in the corner
of New Hampshire The daylight itself is swallowed every afternoon
at the far end red as an apple poured down a throat like mulled cider
None of it is true Were we doing as we were told already Or can it
happen without a threatening example of gaining by almost losing
Just by the grip of realizing you are capable of holding the knife yourself
The real terror may be daylight and night dreams merely a rest from it

CRITICAL MASS

Take a place like Horseheads New York named for remains,
transformed from a once peaceful location to carnage,
or people under-experienced, but in famous ways. Gary or Florence,
maybe average students in Oregon or Indiana. We've forgotten.
Today I picked *pools* instead of *leaves* from the screen saver
and chose nine knots of complexity that made the Nile brown,
then red, then cyanotic, followed by the longest lace-edged
meander in extraordinary rose.
There are so few great ideas, so many mediocre, or worse,
the average collects until catcalls asking next door for Friskies
become shouts: a sudden whirlwind of migrating arrivals
and the extraordinary children with rhyming names, loose horses
looking for their mythical fathers in the sea, extra gold eyes.
I know I remember so much more just by being in the yard.
Each thing reminds me stories by their presence: centipede ferns,
the loved dog coiled in the ground story, the bat tree unknown
till we cut it down, wasp dragging a spider who couldn't lift it
and couldn't let it go, mantis eggs, her unforgettable dress
put aside by the sea wall, all the lavish in common.

WIND CHILL

I take the blue blanket from U-Haul the color of the title
portion of the Field Guide to the Atlantic Seashore
to wrap the PVC water pipe hoping to save it from splitting.
I attempt to influence my luck by doing it with outward gladness.
What can it hurt.
Things are about to shrink anyway. Even the bird of brushmarks
in the silver frame will go from Cooper's to Sharp-shinned
in one afternoon and the tub surround will pull away
shrinking from drywall in the old bathroom where we found poetry
and philosophy past workmen had written on lath
before handing them over to the secret dark.
Maybe it's their way of keeping in touch
as if surgeons might stitch notes on your heart before closing.
Imagine houses as libraries full of words waiting for repair.
One started with *the moon a cold classical accident.*

BREATHING WITHOUT EXHALES

This is unbearable we say while doing just that,
reading our lips as if the shapes settled like letters,
like waxwings on a branch baseline.
Nothing is lost from the lines or the photographs.
No amount of reading wears them away, lips or no lips,
jambs or iambs looking so similar in lower case.
The cathedral is upheld, stone humming, ribs vaulting,
insinuation and insulation at the same time.
Credo, I believe, and dado, how meaning interlocks
with stones as the birds settle into the limestone cornice.
Some things inside-out as Gothic, outside-in as socks,
wrong-sided Red-winged blackbird, Black-winged
red bird, tanagers the idea-mirror is held up to.
Las alas, las olas. I write out love to you in flying words,
leaving like water. It settles on my hand on your hip.
I can hardly stand it I say while standing it.

THE BEGINNING

Starting with splendid skin and dark gums
in which small teeth nested like gems in a Mughal necklace,
the poor savant who told weather for any day in history
but could not dress himself, was demo-ing again.
October 11 AD 2004 ? —Overcast he says.
Probably God blocking light with his retinue
in the Irish backyard of the Bishop of Usher.
I can almost remember it myself
like the past lives of which I am capable easily as future ones.
Damp matter coming together at ten a.m.
Animals fully formed and steaming before wandering off
dazed and confused.
The once and next world invented, then denied
to a few wealthy Egyptians whose dust was a cloud
out of west Texas on February 3, 1952.
At any minute a thousand storms worldwide,
equaling reports of gods appearing to the dim-witted,
a ceramic army waiting under the hills of China.
May 2, 1050, in an anecdotal wind, the harp arrived in Ireland.
1302, nove Gennaio, Dante exiled prophetically from Florence
in light rain and a rising Arno.

HOLDING YOUR HORSES

In missing there is a sense like hearing a faint sound
almost lost like a key turning in buckshot down a hall
I presume an internal sense of completeness
in all things as much for Jan Jackson as for her horse
whose time on the vet's table was a dream
with one flat side The doctor said it was perforated
and leaking like a tea ball urgent and in Latin

Waking in her room between sleep and gas bills
she saw a bare leg stick out from the covers
like a bloodless fracture In her dream she had just moistened
two fingers and pinched a wick and the light had fizzled
into a tendon that became the close end of one of the muscles
of the night that whinnied and flexed in its field
and though not surviving ran again in its new dark pasture
coming to no one   not for apples   not for oats

RELUCTANT

The body is never out of style,
             unlike some frescoes in Bologna.
The earth never stops roasting and freezing by turns.
There are always the poles of diaphysis
and epiphysis of the long bones, for those who have them.
             Reluctant to let go, we might try on a funeral
or two as a last chance.
If we can't keep the body, maybe just the heart
like Egyptians in small jars.

And maybe by staring one might see a wisp
lighten the body, as dreams may evaporate
from the muscleless condition of paradoxical sleep,
             that the portion of the horse we are born with,
cauda equina, might be set free in the pasture,
while the rest of the body is removed by the back door,
serenely and with flowers,
             perhaps painted and dressed atmospherically,
as might Masaccio.

ARRIVING FULL-SIZED

As the writer writes, the cool room warming
slowly by human heat, the intrinsically solo
looks out from a house with glass eyes,
each glance starts over like history solving itself.
Last night a dream had a back door
to a hillside clumped with jessamine, forsythia,
hummingbirds and mist. My breaths came in order
of seniority. I expected another in the weeds
emblematic as Altdorfer's billboard afloat
above the panoramic battle of Alexander and Darius at Issus.
I counted smiling as the cause of rivers near the eyes,
but tears overflowed them as words described water,
and I entered it again knowing the leeches in Minnetonka
would come to me like ticks at Letchworth.
When I am away, the house by the water is smaller,
an exhale. As I come home it breathes deeply.
Arriving full-sized we begin all over.
It half-lidded, me holding dreams, starting from zero,
door after door.

THE NEED TO EXPLAIN

People are so interesting, the black lab thinks
who comes earnestly to visit with her ball.
What can I do for her, the usual petting and baby talk,
rake, pick driftwood, discuss the perils of the vertebrate body
starting with symmetry and how we try to explain everything
through that one fact. How it's what we're good at, skewing
to our benefit every interpretation including ultimate origins
—as if we'd know—like how all this started with one guy
and a gust of wind, not a woman to be seen
except as an incubator, and we got away with it.

Or how we presume continuity, suppress any change
too rapid, explain the comfort of repetition,
how I can never hear Corelli or Walkin' Blues too often,
how the government discusses the *scheme* of things
without ever admitting the scheme part,
how we allow no heaven for animals, sorry, or describe
what it was like to be immune until recently,
not to be afraid of sunlight, water and air for the first time
and willing to predict the end from a tongue's poor color,
have a fragment of everything but skepticism pass through
any moment, a thread through a jeweled button.
She is thinking sure, but first just throw it and I'll bring it back.

ONE DAY IN TEXAS HISTORY

when Austin-born Mrs. Jones stepped out for a message,
Mike McCoy, who came in his pants when Missy kissed him,
tried to get most of the people in the row along the window
to faint, since they had the widest aisle.
Seven deep breaths, sink to a knee-bend, then hold your nose
while blowing and rise slowly.
By the time they were upright, three of the five
had a muffled silence surround them like the flooding Brazos.
They crumpled like Santa Anna's troops after a volley.
The plains around San Jacinto lifted to meet them.
Howie missed the ledge by inches.

Sound/light in the same sense as space/time, closed over them
they said, a dimming diminishing, as if the world entire
came to a point, like a living pencil that stopped writing
consciousness and lifted from the page.
Before Mrs. Jones reentered the room we had glimpsed details
of poignancy as clearly as the shapes of soap film deforming on a wire,
seen how, counter to intuition, a sweeping movement of recognition
formed a bubble from it, like Sam Houston saw the Republic of Texas
fully developed instead of a flat platter of detergent moon,
that we were captured by our bodies, how the wind in a gust might separate
feathers of a mockingbird and we glimpse the heart-breaking
tiny and pathetic body inside. Or anoxia, stating the limits of rebellion.

UNDER OATH

When my grandfather, who had only the day before
axed the head off a chicken
and let it run ragged till dead dry in the driveway,
came at me with a switch
on a dead run, shouting blood as I was playing pioneer
and axing with an oar the young maple he planted,
I saw between strokes the end of imagination,
and would have said it then, but was struck dumb:
I'm sorry. I promise
to abandon the ground level fixity of purpose,
making things worse. I promise
to undo the mildewed grout of the worse for wear,
to improve from erosion, corruption, gangrene and mischief.
I promise to reform North America,
profess the inheritibilty of guilt and sorrow for Hiroshima
that will come later in '44,
regardless of who prevails militarily. I promise
on the stellar interiors, mitochrondria, ionized trails
in the atmosphere, the galvanized tub of my wading pool.
I promise not to misuse the past or the future
if I should have one.

LIVING IN MINUTES

There are less of course, and longer, things lasting and not.
Surprisingly a boot, they tell us, touching ice,
melts it slightly from pressure.
Unable to define a moment, there is this,
made longer by anxiety:
I can hardly go a cold foot on wallpaper
before the same oddly out of place flowers pop up again
like incessant reminders,
ahistorical, regardless of seasons, forget-me-nots, recitative.
Fast as that happened,
you are breathing in a hedge-maze. Right now, some are trying
not to have Pluto reduced to an ice ball,
remain as a planet in our minds, not satirical flies teased into a galaxy.
Already there are stars and planets in my speech. In my breaths
I hear periods written as raindrops,
pauses as fishes, dashes as fences. Soon an implied world is there
quick as recognition, small boats in and out of a harbor.
All this happens even driving to work, remarking on lattice, on traffic,
on the softening mountains of North Carolina.
At the end of each observation a stone, implied footprint of a fly.
After an asterisk falls, there is yet another explanation,
the one we made up momentarily to fit the facts.

WHAT BELONGS

If you take them by thousands from Surinam
or the orange backrivers of Asia, they will continue in your aquarium,
but diminished, as bad news we come to think novel or quaint.
Not oblivious to place, they are merely unable to tell you
they shouldn't be there, and you can't see it.
I am thinking of the pink pearly Arawana in the New Orleans restaurant
that moves slowly like a pennant in oil, too long furling in the light,
every motion beautifully deliberate and prolonged. Its trail lingers
like the tail behind a flashlight searching for whereabouts,
lost and irretrievable. Or the lionfish, splendidly ragged reef ivy,
bluer the deeper, but seven within twelve miles
right in the middle of the Florida Panhandle, one in the window
between pizza and discount clothes. In this, self-indulgence has bypassed
respect, distilled wonder to novelty. They are only small dollars
like Discus from Brazil. They move like the caged in perpetual U-turns
and ovals, the sad shapes of captivity. These are immoral and excessive times.
Even the moths that live here openly throw themselves willfully
and desperately against the lights.

AS FAR AS

ten miles out where the Gulf erupted with pewter fish
like sparrows, and farther
where it appeared the blunt sky touched water with electricity,
a seam, she touched him at the edge of promises.
Back on shore, birds in a tree shape turned sideways in a bank,
vanishing, an instant Fall.
Then the bridge frowning and separating from the road, an animal
suddenly facing two lights:
a man behind a wheel, wheels under his aspirations, moving too fast,
the moping hill beyond which red eyes blistered:
the shirt that felt the heart and no farther, skin wild-eyed,
the sink they could see from the bed, its maddening drip,
temperatures peaking and falling like a road with a possum on it,
the shower that rained in one room:
the boy dropped off at the forest which has no horizon but is continuous
green inches while his father went to Food World which orbits the sun,
for the strawberries of his youth gone forever but through him:
pollen of mangos delivered by bats, wings like oar locks,
lights from the toxic or allergic, two towns close together,
petals and craters, hair-do's, prom dresses, proteins,
kisses on reliable eyes.

WHAT *REFILL* MEANS

Down to the last drop and writing in the shadow of my hand
in the Eveready beam after Erin took the lights, I think *refill*,
but once I start in, it's not so easy. There are the Manichaean texts,
split limbs, slug stars like ball dresses swirling off sideways
as if special creations were just by-products of simple recognitions,
planktonic funnels in the after-action of an oar (two when done smartly)
filling the moment, sending expectation's silver knife forward.
Just getting up from the permanent washable lily of the chair,
I step into parsley, mop-tree shadows, into heavy lettuce
of the too-damp air, crickets and stridulators sifting their gravel screens
like Pat in Italy digging for Etruria. Walk past all-sized flowers,
some rehearsing fruit, some merely accepting of the pitiable duration
of life, a dark door closing, an annoyance, a hoodoo, a grateful waste.
Among them I hear the internal sayers of *How can you Why should we*
I find deer hooves, broken-hearted feet, and see how in the soft earth
they still find their way apart from their bodies like wandering good-byes,
like the purpose of fragrance we smother in ignorance, and pretending
not to be prejudicial still say *suspected* and *alleged* when we know better.
I know I get up from the chair in the secret acre refilled by the chance
of seeing, like this morning, a Red-eyed Vireo, an albino roach
importantly repulsive, by just knowing they are all there, already pictured
sideways in guidebooks. It means nothing empty for long,
nothing runneth over, nothing saved.

SOLEMN EXAMPLES

A man in Elvis glasses plays on TV decoration and melody
in a see-through shirt, and in my reading Thomas Moone,
a carpenter on Drake's third voyage, takes his augur to sink
again his own bark *Swan* on his admiral's order.
It is well-known to us spirit is not un-substance but at least
half light, as those having seen through them say, like a curtain
and subject to gravity as when the ghostly mylar balloons
in Safeway after only a few days start descending to the floor,
earth is so compelling.
We are told our spirits must be lifted and relifted like sick things
propped up for a sip of water, hence constant revivals in the South,
what someone from there called a leak in the law of averages.
And when I read to them out loud yesterday what I'd been thinking
I felt it was a private moment to which a microphone had been invited
for our own good as a helping angel for just that room.
Its speaker voice bringing plain facts close to the floating upolstery.
Not to be anecdotal but alive in the air of the lecture room when I said so.
A cool piano. Another sinking bark settled down in a bay off Ecuador.
Balloons again heading for the high fluorescents. And not to be myth,
the literature in which your heroes always win, or another rerun
where you hope maybe this time it could be different, but so real
you whisper to no one, to the screen—wait—don't step into that
dead woman's room.

LASTING IMPRESSIONS

Look at the slight valley of the horse between haunch and shoulder,
recalling its rider and the low hills between. Form never forgets.
Though they are free to be real horses not obscured by work,
not pull anything, they must think hard to do nothing but remember
their lovers to run the low hills and dream and eat up green landscape.
He thinks of her and the way part of him still sinks down the cushions
when he's gone. A few remembering shapes linger till the foam or feathers
take a deep breath and remember what they were. If he comes back soon
he may not be quite missing, indentations rising as if still getting up.
When he leaves he feels her still on him, a loving cinch like the feel of hat,
the hat gone.

COSMOLOGY

OK, there was the sky woman and the earth man,
there was the original snake and the three fire stones,
stars as a river and strewn coals;
there was everything from nothing, from three or four
elements to more than a hundred with the theoretical
metaphors of shepherds from herding peoples,
fish from fishers, kings from cats,
world as a flat circle with a bowl over it marked with stars,
figures of the dead watching for failures;
there was the monkey in a tree that came down
to be us on the grand savannas
that gave us sore backs, the couple in a garden asked to leave
from some of the same presumptions of innocence
and ignorance,
all the stories of something using a language with no words
for what it really is, or even that you could know it,
determine the true past from here,
that whatever we suggest, there is always something
behind it, or beside it, or many at the same time. Mythology
is a caster for the mind, a cushion like a rubber cup
under the sofa to protect the floor.
That is why we can't get there, why sacred and scared
are anagrams of each other.

BACK TO US LAST NIGHT

All this is biography,
some of it auto, some manual, much of it
laughing within a shirt.
The dust reads back to us last night
as soon as it settles.
The edges of footprints weather with time
and destination.
As they do, the rest pass by without ever
touching down.
This is concentration, untangling the brainstem
thread by thread.

The bone moon, the single thumb print,
sometimes partial, sometimes full,
maybe enough to be traceable, the sky
handled like worry beads.
Everything we touch leaves prints.
We can be tracked back where we came from.
Some of us comes off on the furniture,
some on time.
It takes all night to recover.
Only the little compact of light
that came through two rooms to rest on the dresser
was for sure. Things have their reasons.
Black-paged albums stare back at us
like our room at night.

HOW FOLKLORE STARTS

It was during the year when masterpiece was not impossible
but increasingly unlikely—this one—when I heard the announcer
say William Berg's Mass for Three Horses instead of three voices.

At the time I thought, fabulous, this could turn everything around.

The beautiful oven of the August Gulf is seen best from Wisconsin.
Too much hot metal to touch, too many hopes heaped on impossible,
the clippings of which are faded and worn through from your wallet.

A good title but hopeless when I heard them actually harmonizing
not like horses at all, but rhymes like little bells ringing in words
to no purpose but attention to themselves, scaffolds, not Appaloosas.

What more could be done to prepare that story.

After currying, grooming, dressing for dinner in new shoes,
something swirls offshore in overheated uncertainty. You can hear hooves
in the gathering clouds, pawing to begin, a fugue in alternating names.

SIDE EFFECTS

I had not noticed that the black was blue,
that statues had fallen silent and emptied their eyes,
the little gems unglued.
I had been walking all day with different socks, slightly uneasy,
sometimes one-legged, with a dream as crutch.

Dark on the starless ceiling the earth rolls under
whose angels are blades struck from a flint core.

But for TV it could have been years before anyone
called for a suicide, saying I am precarious, I soften in my hands.

Passion is a place like a mixture of wavelengths.
Water and fire share its moods.

So the ocean was giving back blue, while black was its inner hallelujah.
Sun on the edges of the stems of daisy fleabane
was copper wires wrapped on a rotor, awaiting ignition.
The nine-minute light from the star that balloons and shrinks,
is shredded by the fence.

Some death is needing these details, and dice, and maniacs.

SAD FACTS

From the unmistakable garden of good reasons
for inventory to become narration,
the azalea opens its corolla to the flies and spiders,
the dogwood gives up its denizens:
wood borers, tongue worms, ants.

Children heal quickly as they do everything.
As for the rest of us,
our wounds are remarkably low in oxygen,
high in traumatic acids.

The person unable to write anything may sing,
explaining what is damaged.
The stutterer sings. The heart murmurs,
then speaks. The words are recorded.
There are gaps and glitches in the tapes.

If the words are changed the landscape withers.
We will have no nostalgia for the farm.
We will separate like seeds and cease believing.
We will stand back telling two stories at once,

how things in good order are anxious for tomorrow,
how some things do not continue, cannot
as corn cannot reseed without us,
increasing the list of things we have made helpless.

And what of this: the calf in the pasture
that became a flowered purse, a shoe.

JUST IN TIME

The first time I was the center of something
it was freezing.
Vowels glittered like snow banks, the Amboys
gold on silver at that hour.
Like the antique spoon, my remarkable molecules
were birds of the sun,
morning doves reading aloud from their delicate laments,
most of their flyway through my chest
in coughs. I was seven in Minnesota just in time.

This morning it all came back in the few minutes
between electricity and springs,
between the numbers constructed of straight lines
and the hands that swept the face,
like Marigold smoothing her dress between morning
and downtown.
In those small minutes the future could be confused,
an unthinking arrow
passed through the body of a cygnet, then a swan.

THE APPEAL OF ANTIQUES

The intriguing comfort of an imagined past
is entered through objects
the same way we continue the present
but without nostalgia
Parents so long for happiness they say
one life is not enough
and live through their children
But children also live backwards through past candles
crank telephones carriages
the ascendant animals that lived not in imagination
but in Kansas and before
there was an Oklahoma with its spotted sun

In those days a metaphor for Hell was the corn sheller
field corn shriven shooting out cobs
the grindstone razor strop even the ladder of progress
from which Les Westfield slipped
on a mossy rung though his son held the ladder
and fell two stories:
one the feudal structure of the family two the harmonic
of almost fatal necessity
as the maple stump entered his hip along with the difficult
remission of breath itself
an antique whose furious elaborations mimicked the rose

HABITS

Any wild place alone is exhilaration and remorse.
How could we have thought it just lumber and mines.
Now we have the shells of our habits, empty scaffolds
of actions, slow motions that surround healing
like a necessary cleaning of Navona,
the statue's once lucky eyes rolled back, diverting Niagara
to mend its rocks, cementing together the old expectations
that things will stay the way we remember.
But dissociated bodies, heavy as pine log furniture,
spend immense dull hours sitting alone in the same chair
staring. Nothing like this revives.

Then with nothing apparently beyond its own anxiousness,
the first hummingbird appears out of the loon's shiver-call
as if a wavering stone propelled backward out of the sound
of water where it hit, and the shuffling of the velvet deck
of purpose in its wings. Little to withstand such witness,
not the enduring poignancy of a single body in the wind,
not the exuberance of looking into the bird-filled windows
from the outside, love passing through glass. After each
such feeling we can again make promises, a touch, a look,
a *please come* given like handshakes or waving goodbye.
It is then we can lift back up, see the jewels in our throats.

SUSPENDED ANIMATION

Like the TV dark but always on,
needing only one touch like love to its key pad
to become conscious of late-breaking news,
and people kissed awake from sleeping,
peering fearfully over the gunnels to a manganese pond
seeing only their heads like worn sheets fluffed out
over a futon for unexpected visitors,
remorse is latent but awake to the show dogs,
cut to conform to our ideal,
to the work-song mules who would die for us,
working to our voices.

Tonight the moon has a last name,
that's how well known it is. But it's really a half moon,
and its back is turned, and it's not its real name,
just the one we gave it. In the world of advertising,
we have the happy animals sing themselves to slaughter.
At Beach Barbecue, the menu pigs dance into their sandwiches,
lobsters like Louganis dive smiling on the boiling stove.
We take comfort. We take Bossie to the flashing knives.
We are remote. We skip where their names are written in
by another advertiser, another loathed forest backed against the glass.
No wonder the faces flutter. No wonder water
rings down its milfoil curtains.

SPONTANEOUS COMBUSTION

First, stories like those told at camp in dark cabins,
then photos arrived of cinders and a leg in a shoe
by a fireplace, a scorched chair as if lightning had clapped
and hit entirely inside a corner of a London flat,
or a demon needed light for a dark errand and used her
like a wick till it finished playing back-lash
and circles-in-the-pans, or maybe drawn to the odor
of leek soup, entered the apartment through her like a fuse.

This is how they pass from one interest to the next,
say the most eager to believe. Pale Edith spoke cheerfully
all day on the telephone and after work tried a sixth suicide,
this time with fire. Carlo da Bolsano, figlio, arrives
from Africa with news of the pangolin, an arboreal tiled cat
that hangs by its tail and appeared to him on a termite ball
like a flared angel.

The common is next to impossible, the vicarage next to that,
and to all the combustible records of the perigees and apogees
kept in the same drawer. For the more reluctant, he demonstrated
how unseen forces are with us. Touching magnet to parchment,
iron shreds haloed themselves in broad daylight.

NOTIONS FROM THE EAST

When the rain grows up the cyclones spin
like roses on radar. We name them. They answer.
In fact the clouds have been signaling for years
—danger—the weather is sharpening something
you can hear in the islands first.
We had thought they were atmospheres, not friends.
Not life like a birthday with storm candles aflame
in the toasty Caribbean, cloud tops, cakes
with their own knives, not with that singe.
What I thought black was blue. Flat refraction,
conclusions mapped in orthogonals, vain lords
black and unanimous.

So the impacts were written verse-visa
and numb in the eyes. Ripples don't last
unless water smiles around the island
from a long fetch, looking for coastlines,
self-sorting in the quiet by your feet.
All it takes are differing densities and the water moves,
the north goes south darker than me, fish-twisted,
with the Coriolis forming a hill above resentment
and the relict sediments. Then down-sloped with frictions
and you have psychology from a lingering wind,
and river discharge resulting in outbursts and islands
of clothing strewn around the room.

SWAN SONG

Swan song I supposed was an elaborate achievement
like a honey locust large as the county, each leaf tied on
purposely with decorative whipping, until I learned
it meant the end—words like cracked paving
leading down to the beckoning edges of Lake Harriet.
It is not my job to explain this, but some are mute.
Beautiful autists whose necks could reach newcomers
through a fence if they were careless, or the bottom
of the pond, and we could see their soundless machinery,
black feet moving with the grace of cats, the first sign
ever they were plain like us and not ethereal.

I must have been ten in a long past Minneapolis,
when the streetcars with yellow wicker seats traveled
downtown tying a cord around the lakes as if they were
drawstring reticules, when one night someone or two
swam out to their island nest and cut their throats.
The city went dark as lake water. Breast feathers
floated off like ultimogeniture. Later came the films
of the terribly burned animals from near ground zero
being loaded into trucks, their eyes wide as explosions.
Who are we. What sick creation makes mute angels
live among demons.

WITNESS TO INCREASING PERIL

Eric our checker has Conformity
Is Suicide tattooed
on his forearm as a footnote for life.
He rings up the lemons
and bouquet and flashes his attitude
in flesh text
while under him his shadow makes fun.
First a rhino as he swipes.
A dwarf sideways behind his back.
Traditional fluorescents working against him.

There is nothing in the myths anymore
just this over and over.
And there is conformity. There is witness
to increasing peril.
There is spending just to go fast. Double-bagging
opinionated hopes.
But no energy's left in the Don't Look Back,
the ruined man
twisted to a stick, waking up from death
like a nap mistaken,
the always assumption of Something More,
especially for us.
And if you have it, what do you have.
And then what.

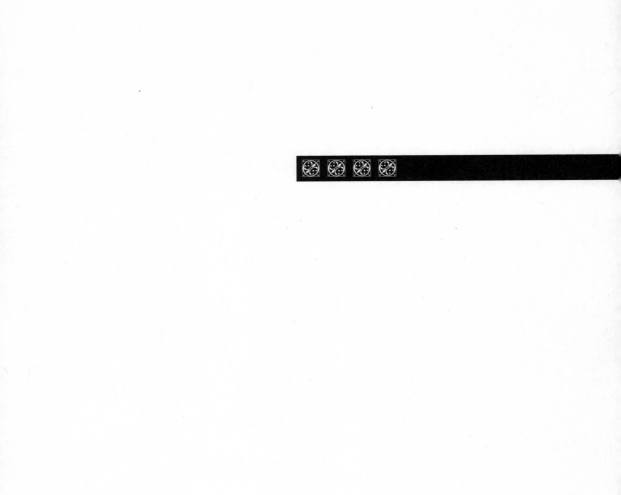

I'LL TAKE IT FROM HERE

No one ever says it is a *journey*
as they might of life, the churning within.
That is a literary word.
We might use *travel*, but we are not going anywhere
in the ordinary sense.
There is no distance rolling by, no landscape
being dragged past the window.
It is more the feeling of movement when you're not,
as the blue and white whirling skirts
of brushes pass you by in the car wash's
stationary tour of the seasons.

This morning opens on water and electrolytes,
magnesium from green vegetables,
salt of course, or shock in its absence.
Passing like nothing to hide,
it flings plumage, nomenclature, fragments of alphabet,
gold around the eye of the frilled lizard.
Even I am changing under myself,
my philanthropic cells
patriotic where the assembling "I" is the patria.
A process of which I know nothing
until a fever, a conflict in digestion, a dream girl
resplendent in polysaccharides and fats
marries a shy bone that comes and goes like fan mail.
I have an idea, integument under its own power.
I have another: I am wrong.

BEFORE THE AFTERLIFE

Windburn is sleeping in the rain like the radical attitudes of Boston
tucked in the general populace
Nowhere is consequence more sufficient or on time
I would give up my ibids for more

Vivian who was certain of obstinate denial found a hibiscus
closed around a bee
bobbing on the stem like a pink sleeping car then falling
while she watched

In the Lion's club formerly a church collectors of Lionels laid out
branches and veins
They made a Chicago out of the chapel For a dollar you could watch
restricted destinies
passengers and logs through small towns and reindeer moss

In the ritual expectation of death is first a stiffness
then senseless bones
begin to move like exuberant freight So much of the business
of the afterlife is dancing after naps
as they have it in the manuscripts of nuclease and travel

The bodies snooze on in the little Pullmans No more in love than usual
Rich in torments Gathering speed

FORENSICS

A polite and practical breeze spreads field flowers.
An ermine comes through headed for the king's coat sleeve.
Not likely.
But how easy it is to cause the impossible from raw materials.
Numbering the bones for recognition later, tracking down one bacterium
with a crippled whip. Bringing the gist to justice.

Which is the yellow made from urea, which from chrome.
Yes, there are specialists. Wind just mentioned, opening the way
to the drone on the keeled flower,
emptying the beach pea of its butter daubs in the acceptable story,
the new bride given, then unwrapped, from her satin package in another, less so.
What sickness. And what do they mean *given*.

Enter the symbionts, the complicitous, the prelates who choose them.
Enter a whalebone Mary you are supposed to admire, only locked and frozen.
Not easy.
Of course, you don't have to prove anything. Each day the ink blots read
differently. Sound separates from action after 30 meters, film slows to jerks.
You won't be able to explain those deaths in the hills above Srebrenica,
what hatreds are paying back. And what do they mean *paying*.

We only find this much: Tears make poor snowflakes because of minerals;
ermines are just weasels in the Spring.

HEROIC PROPORTIONS

Wing beats attracting males
                    make even the bare walls hungry
There was to be a wedding so they fixed the fountain
and the courtyard
took on the focus of a flower but enlarged
                    Fountain the pistil white chairs
flocked like pollen
windows and roofline crinkled into Spanish formality
at the Best Western Granada
as snowflakes form around particles
                    dust a new star

For us symmetry is dignity
                    and so the words spoken at the apex
of one-point perspective are a spell of assurance
                    The air organized to song by the hired DJ
sets up celebrity
in the atrium like a heart for a period of hours
                    Satins start appearing
lace and nine white teaspoons—bridesmaids—
                    their pathway crystallized with name cards

I think love arises from complexity
well above the wasps
                    so we love its forms the very idea
that organization is iconic and effective
at the vanishing point
                    where light scares shadows off the floor

GOING GOOSEFLESH

We are becoming something else at all times
       As when the pile driver quit
sending bridge beams into the silt of the bottom at five
       and it took dreamlike minutes for the echoes
to end as background in the minds of the affected
       who began to look up from the Dialogs of Plato
baiting another hook to realize how long their bodies
       had been listening and gradually modifying
their inner rhythms to the power of the weight
       of a Volvo steam-lifted and dropped
       lifted and dropped
a meditation both borrowed and ignored
       and how if this had continued long enough
they might have ended up wholly otherwise
       how two limbs rubbing are a saddle in the trees
an E-minor triad and some go gooseflesh
       This is why newlyweds go to water white noise
to a falls to work against dismal Miltons
       and those taking comfort from the theory the universe
blew up and will again
To be able to say simply looking up from assuring clamor
       I love you I am so little what I was

THOSE WERE THE DAYS

Often as moss I stare at my hands in amazement,
at the what I'm made of,
the coming into being, the abiding and changing,
the nostalgia for the gone.
And I am lonesome too for the too small to see,
where the hair on my hand
is a walk in the Smokies, skin starred and strewn
with Chryslers, cumulus
adrift in my nails, or cloudless like ten open windows
to the blood.

More than half through my minus summation, nineteen
forty to some vague emptiness up the road
preceded by a dash, indicative of getting there too fast,
blur between two years,
complimentary arson in one mark. Those were the days,
are. At some point
down the economies, pictures disappear from motel walls,
soft tissues, extra shampoo.
Soon you will be in an almost empty room of your own making
pacing off days, undistracted
by vases of peonies or seascapes, gold skies outside.

A FORECAST

Frances says the alfalfas are using the road
this year for migration
and I have seen an ovenbird with novas on its chest
and threatening storm clouds
moving across the bodies of Holsteins in addition
to those they had originally
like the moon that looks in on us like family
now that we've been there

My room opens its three eyes on the urgent
rush of the pittosporum
and schefflera pressed against the glass
in fear of the hurricane
I can hardly see water for their frantic hands

This week there is no Friday
Everything is cerrado but the wrens As a comfort
I turn on the lights
so they can sympathize and I can practice the idea
of writing as a private act

Every day brings the well-dressed weather women
predicting futures
supplying possibilities indicating whether or not
we are wearing transparent
through our hearts imagining the endless and otherwise
beyond us with the watery
tools of daydreams and spider silk gun sights
all alone one hand wishing the other

HYDROLOGY

If you know hydrology you can visualize the beautiful
fluid chaos in the heart,
vigorous music in four apartments overlooking Central Park,
liquid hydrangeas, mums.
In the classes of nutrients there are bread and ideas.
The commonest will feed us.

Where bubbles will start in a heating pan,
how we fished near the channel marker. The great dull Reds
and inquisitive Ling
who live in hydrology were drawn to the mechanical
heart of the engine.
In the heart of the water, the tide re-decides every few hours
to run in the other direction,
the earth and the moon fighting over it.

Look at your money. No one is smiling.
This is the message of symbolism trapped by constriction.
Fear runs faster. A boat against light chop
full throttle is shuffling cards to people listening, chances.
The ocean has bones in it, but they belong to others.
Its muscles are theirs.
Its eyes, and the heart of it, the heart like digging out
spadeful by spadeful, you hear
with your head on her chest, the advantageous fluid that waits
behind the faucet and the eyes.

NO PERHAPS

The moon is on. Lights are, at home,
down deep in the wires.
Ladies in golf hats float above grass beds,
dancing shrimp like puppets
for sea trout and flounder.
Iced wine coolers drift on a string by the bait bucket.
Elsewhere the poet was asked about his age.
His assumption was night
is closer to death than daylight and 40 closer than that.
His birthday was tomorrow.

But that is only the national average.
A current could deaden a wet hand any hour,
take those ladies toasting fishes to an endless noon,
or out through the pass to the ocean
to waltz within a wreck.
Or a truck may come calling dragging a loose disturbance
in the light behind, and a crumpled one in front.
Death has its own accounting. It adds by feel.

A crab is a Braille creature,
one is reading the littoral last night in front of me.
It says we must stop
thinking of this as scenery.
It's one hundred and we sit in the arid wind,
the oldest of all of us, having flashbacks
the electric gifts of reason.
There is no perhaps.
The ladies are reliving. The lake is stay put,
a river is pass through. Everything aging as it can.

FAULT ZONE

When the upheavals happen, deep noise under us,
some dread pooling in the ears,
we recall the most frightening, irreconcilable news:
We are flammable. We are too fat and can
go up like magma through synclines, spew igneous
minerals, basalt under continents, sputtering candles,
burn. With no skin, we leak.

Paul's number was the same as the year Cook arrived
in Hawaii's hot islands, threatening everything.
The charts of the day showed tragedy
arrived in all sizes, and the candle fingers sat
with the captain to plan them, reminding the windows
how mountains moved aside, though not fast enough.

Then, as if an island, a boat in the harbor
below Pele, attacked by inhabitants,
Elsbeth's incense candle caught and her office went up,
hibiscus to acrid melt within an hour.
Sometimes there is no point in trying to pull things together:
continents broken, fly ash from the lungs,
Jack from the trash fire that discolored and claimed him,
who had a hose and ocean and did not use them.

JUNE IN THE INNER EAR

Each time chemo asked, she answered with handfulls
of sunny hair. It didn't matter
she pinched up her cheeks for the radiologist,
none of this showing up on film.
Everyone has stories of a loved one, a relative with
an earthquake under an ear,
an island appearing like a sesamoid, where tendons
of longing sawed.
The ocean is breathing for everything in it. Skinless
it shows its heart.
They dive for it, dark and ischemic below the whales.

Still each month is like a Doge-in-waiting,
readied magnificence, palaces of May with puff sleeves
and June in the inner ear, lush
with accumulated sounds, arenous riverbeds, ephemera.
Organizing outs around dialysis and coma,
in deep bad dating with those machines.

Long enough is up to the symptoms courting the muscles
and the mind, the least of these
leading to the body becoming horizontal and soft.
In amplexus and the mall,
we are watching each other for signs who will give up
wisdom for the dark,
whose hair might fill a whole room, who flourish with a nurse.
There are precedents,
the amputee museums, rooms of marble figures, few intact.
They are too pale
an exaggeration, but we need them, the hard smiling histories.

THE NATURE OF FORGIVENESS

The nature of forgiveness is like dispersing ice
with gunfire. Everything remains
as the echo evaporates,
   a gesture without effect.
It is the heat that riddles it like worms.
An inability occurring hugely at the poles
though locally strong in the vodka tonic
   and the effect we have on others.
Little lasts. Nothing you can be sure of,
   good acts, kindness.
I have known and forgotten so many. Anyway,
who is rehearsed for such massiveness,
   same for sorries.
So what can it matter, forgiveness,
me there riddled like spring ice, wind-bent
in my little box,
   all our trees murdered for houses,
our houses demolished for the sake of ridding the future
of the past.
   In the ilex, a starling murmurs to itself
so melodically and soft, it is clearly personal.
   The magics of everyday have no regrets.
In this one, the bird that seems coarse to so many
purrs as it searches,
   its secrets private, its innocence ignored.
In numbers, communities use shotguns and cherry bombs.
   Still, they remain dark and reluctant
like the vast unrepentance of water.

SHRINKING TO PINPOINTS

Things we love best have backbones
but leave us.
Visitors shrink to live in the pinpoints of perspective.

Years ago we were given the suite of seasons
like a large hotel.
The rooms we inhabited changed color
like the orange afternoons that mentioned evening
down the hall,
morning as the blood surrounds us.
Downstairs in childhood the lobby was all sunlight
and sexual palms.

Eggs in the ovules, fish in the freezer, dentine dressed in enamel.

When the five boats entered the lake in New Hampshire
to shoot the swans, the residents realized the door had been opened
to the unforgivable.
The men from the so-called Wildlife Service
who carried off the dead said it was necessary, they were so destructive
of habitat.
Look who's talking said everything else.

Exit the Craniata, just visitors, into the pinpoints.
Exit the feathered reptiles in our hands,
checkout by twelve.
Welcome bacteria, with discounts for the unseen
autotrophs, spores and sponges,
things that go on swimmingly despite us.

I SWEAR

Now it's only me and the no-see-ums,
    bull gnats in the slow-pitch baby talk of the South,
rain-soaked nicknames and diminutive wing music.

Now the Sound is flat lacquer, a foregone conclusion
    of the windless bay with back talk, a single cylinder
shrimp-engine reluctantly tipping them off,
    an emergency like yesterday's, blood red,
turned over and over by the earth like a smooth carnelian.
    An insect brings a siren to my ear.

Morning repeats like a child the same question.
    I look back and the path from last night has overgrown
behind me. I can see nothing of its tracks despite my quarters
    though I turn on my atlas like the observation binoculars.
In no time squash vines covered the compost
    but put out a melon because I was wrong about the leaves.
I am one of the practical impractical. I am here now
    raising my temperature in the presence of white horses,
anti-terrigenous clouds with a tail wind, beginning and ending
    in themselves.

Flaming plum, sweet in its pyre, must just burn out
    like the eyelid of sky, napping when I close my own,
nothing practical can save it. But each tide is two half-truths,
    reluctance and resignation, and for those who think aesthetic
and practical are opposites, remember the painters
    mixing velvet and water to restore them.

Congo or River Wye, a sling strung in the triple canopy,
    mowing the sloping pasture or the little waste place
behind the Roadway Inn in Baton Rouge
    with weeds and gas showers, all are homesick
for the here and now, and from a plastic chair in seaside grape
    and spartina I do not say a name, I smile.
That is a whole truth and nothing but.

BUNJI

Music, awareness of the frequency of nerves,
hums inwardly, making preferences so we hear Samuel Barber
and choke up during falling chord changes,
think poignancy is noted in the score rather than a plexus
though they resonate together.

As an alfalfa moth under the schefflera hides in its own light,
we make less of astonishing than it is.

Of course. This is ignorance, our birthright.

I had long hair because I could. Now I have inherited circumstance
and the nerve to jump light-headed from the overpass,
spider on a thread, a neuron-thin river below, both singing pleasure,

passing out ounces as I am lifted and beckoned on the way,
eking mortality.

Whether we cool down from wind or heat up from friction
in free fall is like asking the function of fever,
why the parallel of care is often the impossibility of relief.

Ironic is a stretch between tightening excitement and exhaust.
We can be in the same place and describe it differently,
feel the invisible laboring right behind perception.

Soon we will be back to normal.
Thrumming will have stopped far from where we started.
Fever will have broken. We will be at the end of our rope.

TAKING MY TIME

Scarabs include the rose chafer. Day includes the dark
since ours starts at midnight.
Leaves ward off the sky. Roots are lightning underground
just as humus and rock
are the deliberate come hither of the earth, waiting for us,
turvied, a solid wink of past animals
still carousing in the stone. I can say more. I am in no hurry.

The sun is throwing what designers call peachblow
at the dock twice a day. I turn
the sundial like a goblet to daylight savings to make it last.
I stretch to nine-fifteen.
A book is a record of how someone spent their time.
A heart comes with a hammer
and floodgates. Night is when dead limbs fall on the roof
and plumbing squirms in its sweated joints.

All this and more. Form is its own deliberator, things crackle
and divide like stand-ins,
Ganymede to Jersey. Life is so many flashbacks, I am only
as fast as I thought, often back to Iowa,
the Desoto's floor starter, baby jay fed with a dropper, being high
as a door knob, unable to reach the light.
And flash forwards, when I go to the available scale that tells me
the epicenters, loveseats, my weight upon the moon.

THE
JUNIPER
PRIZE

This volume is the 31st recipient of the Juniper Prize
for Poetry presented annually by the University of
Massachusetts Press for a volume of original poetry.
The prize is named in honor of Robert Francis
(1901–1987), who lived for many years at Fort Juniper,
Amherst, Massachusetts.